Betsy Hearne

By the same author

Home
South Star
(Margaret K. McElderry Books)

Eli's Ghost

Eli's Ghost

Betsy Hearne

illustrated by Ronald Himler

Margaret K. McElderry Books
NEW YORK

Margaret K. McElderry Books
Macmillan Publishing Company
866 Third Avenue
New York, N.Y. 10022
Collier Macmillan Canada, Inc.

Composition by Maryland Linotype Composition Company
Baltimore, Maryland
Printed and bound by R. R. Donnelley & Sons,
Harrisonburg, Virginia

First Edition
Printed in the United States of America

10 9 8 7 6 5 4 3 2 1

Library of Congress Cataloging-in-Publication Data

Hearne, Betsy Gould.
Eli's ghost.

Summary: Eli searches for the mother he'd long assumed
dead in a hugh swamp where he is sustained by the ghosts
of friends from earlier days and where a brush with
death causes his own ghost to leave his body and get
into all the mischief Eli never has.
[1. Ghosts—Fiction. 2. Swamps—Fiction. 3. Mothers
and sons—Fiction] I. Himler, Ronald, ill. II. Title.
PZ7.H3464E1 1987   [Fic]   86-21096
ISBN 0-689-50420-9

For Michael,
friendly presence and
prince of storytellers

Eli's Ghost

1

In the old days, every little southern town was a world of its own, hard to get into and harder to get out of. There were no telephones, flush toilets, or electric lights, but there were plenty of ghosts. Some were friendly and some weren't. In Eli Wilson's case, they were a mixed blessing. He'd heard about ghosts all his life, yet he wouldn't ever have seen any if he hadn't decided to leave home.

The night he ran away it was pitch dark. Eli tried to square his shoulders, but it wasn't easy. They were round to begin with. His chin was strong, though, for a plump face, and his eyes clear of tears. For a few minutes he walked backward away from the high white house on the hill, seeing it as if for the first time, and maybe the last. Then he turned around toward the swamp. Folks said the swamp was so big it could swallow you alive, the swamp was a ghost yard. Still Eli stepped into its first dark reaches. He knew what was behind. He might as well go ahead.

Two shapes followed him to the edge of the swamp. One glowed like a round black pearl. The other appeared as some sharp shadow cast at noon, except the sun had set. Unnoticed from house or hill, they watched Eli as they had watched him through all the years since they had died. Without rightly knowing it, Eli sensed their presence and shivered.

"Lord have mercy," sighed one to the other. "Eli's leaving home."

Sheriff Stone leaned back in his swivel chair and stretched out his short legs to rest on the desk. A fly circled above him, fresh from the mule and wagon tied outside. Sheriff Stone linked his fingers on top of his head right over the bald spot. This way, it appeared he had a lot of hair, and it was his favorite position for thinking.

He was thinking about fishing. Or had been. Now he had to think about Eli Wilson. If people would just stay put and not get into trouble, a sheriff's job would be a lot easier. This was a small town. A body would think people could just keep themselves in one spot. No need for any trouble. Now this boy Eli, gone all night. Never been in any trouble before. A-perfect, according to everybody. Probably couldn't be anything else with old man Wilson breathing down his neck. Mean man, Wilson, mighty mean. Stingy, with just a little twist to the mouth that told a person more than enough to stay away. But rich, with that high white house on the hill. Spooky house, said

to be haunted. Darn fool stories, but most everybody stayed away, whether from ghosts or Henry Wilson was hard to say.

The fly began to buzz louder round Sheriff Stone's head. He batted at it, losing a little of the balance he had practiced through so many years of propping his feet up on the desk.

Maybe the boy was kidnapped. But who? Who around town would dare and who out of town would know? Or maybe he was lost. But he wasn't the kind of boy who wandered around where he wasn't supposed to, or did anything he wasn't supposed to: just school and home again. There were rumors he played with Tater Sims and Lily Tilman, but nobody ever saw them run around together. Just one of those town gossips trying to get even with old Henry Wilson's overcharging everything in his store. No use trying to round up Tater or Lily. Know-nothings, both of them—never even showed up in school. Eli Wilson wouldn't run with a pack of field hands, anyway, not if his pa had anything to say about it.

There was the teacher, Eileen Smith. Maybe she would know something. If she didn't know, she'd sure have an opinion on it. Or maybe one of Eli's school buddies would have some idea of what he'd been up to lately. Better take old man Wilson along over to the school. Just the sight of him would scare a kid's tongue loose.

The thing was, Eli was so dang good. If it was one of those King boys, or the Jacksons, that would be a different matter. They could be out there setting up a still and drinking bad whiskey. But Eli Wilson would be the last person in the world to get in trouble, or put anybody else to any trouble. The boy was naturally, honestly, reliably, truly good. Where he got it from, now that was a puzzle. Certainly not from his pa. And his ma was long gone. Used to be a couple of servants around, was all, of no account, sat around swapping stories day and night. Probably started that whole story about ghosts. But those servants were long dead. Buried somewhere back of the hill, if he recalled right. Henry Wilson would never pay for a proper gravestone.

Eli did have a dog, funny old dog, followed after him like a shadow every time he stepped out the door. But now that's interesting, did the dog disappear with him? If not, something must have happened to the boy, must have fallen in the river or something. Could have slipped off one of those overhangs down by the bridge. Better hunt the river first, then cover the swamp. Boy was forbidden to set foot in the swamp, according to his pa, but he did play down by the river.

That was a sad thought, the river, because disappearing in the river would be the end. Disappearing in the swamp left a little hope, but the boy would never have crossed his pa to go in there. Old man Wilson sure hated that swamp worse than poison. Got all greeny-white in the face even saying how no son of his ever set foot in it.

Living with old man Wilson, come to think of it, might not be much better than disappearing in the river. But the boy was too young to think of that yet. Seemed the kind of child that just lived his life along, minding his own business, what business there was to mind.

Maybe he was hiding out somewhere, though. Maybe the old man pushed the limit and came down on him too hard. In that case he'd come home as soon as he got hungry. Plump, mighty plump little boy. Pale face, near-white hair—just about glinted in the sun—and plump. Big eyes, though, always looked hungry. Just lonesome, like as not. Lonesome eyes. Gray eyes. Always kicking a stone down the road every time a body saw him. Probably just passing along a kick from the old man. Some children turned mean from a bad parent, and some just hurt inside.

Now all this was doing nothing in the way of a search. Better get on with it. Pity, too, with a perfect day for fishing. But duty first. Citizens before catfish. The thing would be to round up old man Wilson, if he'd leave his store long enough to look for his son, go over and talk to the teacher, then round up a few men and search the river. See if there's any talk of strangers been seen poking around. Check all the old sawdust piles around the mill to see if he got buried in a cave-in. Not likely, but known to happen. Happened to the Howard girl a few years back. Spread the word around the county. Cover the swamp. Too bad there weren't some good dogs around. Now that Tracker was dead, there were just those no-account, mangy hunting dogs hanging around Kings and Jacksons. No use setting them on a trail. They'd just as soon tree a cat. Better use the horse and cover ground and see what turns up.

Sheriff Stone played a waiting game with the fly, easing his hand into position for the final swat. Suddenly, he leaned sideways and lunged, felt the chair tip just a hair too far on its right rear leg, and met the ground with a whack. He lay there a moment, his thoughts circling. It was an undignified position, but getting out of it seemed fairly tricky.

If the boy were to turn up alive, there sure wouldn't be much skin left on his back when old man Wilson got finished with him. But on the other hand, a body's got to be strict with these kids. They get away with murder these days. Duty first, they might as well learn right off from the start. Eli Wilson better get his tail back here fast if he's alive, and if he's not . . . well, where would he be?

Sheriff Stone waved his legs awkwardly in the air as the fly zipped out the window.

2

Eileen Smith called her class to order the next day and cast her sharp eyes around for anything amiss. The big thing missing, of course, was Eli, but there was nothing they could do about that. The sheriff had men spread all over the county, and Eli's father was not one to let ground go uncovered when it came to one of his own good name.

Also missing was a tree snake which Lily Tilman had brought in for science on one of her rare days at school. Eileen Smith waved her cardboard fan at the thought of a snake crawling around her classroom.

The class was uneasy. Whenever something like Eli's disappearance happened in a small town, thought Eileen Smith, or in a small class, it took all eyes off work. It preoccupied the minds of everyone because there was so little else to occupy them. Even she felt discombobulated.

There was something very odd about her most regular, most considerate student being absent and un-accounted for. It raised thoughts that she did not want to entertain. What if something had happened to the boy? This was certainly out of the ordinary. Spitballs might fly and pigtails be pulled as a regular procedure of the universe, but Eli was never absent, as far as she could remember, and certainly not missing. That was a thing that did not sit well with Eileen Smith. And evidently not with her class. They were sitting more quietly than usual as if waiting her direction, all eyes turned away from Eli's seat and yet drawn toward it furtively, as if expecting to see him suddenly appear.

They were so quiet that Lily Tilman's tree snake began to unwind from his hiding place behind the empty back desk and think about mouse hunting.

The whole class knew about Eli, of course. The word traveled fast. Newspapers were unnecessary in Wilsonville, always too late. Eli Wilson was missing from his home and in fact had not been seen since dinnertime two days before. The river had been dragged, and the old sawdust piles, which occasionally caved in and buried children jumping or sliding down them, had been searched. Miss Smith was really at a loss for words. Neither she nor the rest of the class seemed able to concentrate, yet there was really nothing else to do. At last she stopped the assignment out of a sense of discomfort—itself an unusual thing—and said simply, "Perhaps there is some way we can help Eli. Does anyone remember anything he said recently, or did, that was unusual? Perhaps someone has overlooked an important item of information, someone here in this class."

There was silence. Eli, in fact, talked to everyone

and no one. He was pleasant, helpful, fair, and determined when necessary but not a friend that anyone shared secrets with—anyone else in class. He was known to run with black Tater and wild Lily, but nobody mentioned it because he was a Wilson, and neither Tater nor Lily came to school much. Lily's mother needed her to take care of the baby boys. Tater lived alone and worked to support himself. Maybe those two knew something, but nobody in class did. Nobody had heard or seen a thing different from usual till the day he didn't show up.

Lily Tilman's tree snake started to weave its way toward the mousehole beside Eileen Smith's desk.

Eileen Smith reflected. The children were always whispering about ghosts on Henry Wilson's hill, of course, but that was all nonsense. Personally, Miss Smith thought the hill and Henry Wilson were both impressive. That was neither here nor there as far as Eli's being gone. It helped to talk about his disappearance, though, Eileen Smith could see that. They had all been tensed up avoiding it, and now some of the worry eased out with the words. They would all just have to wait and see. And meanwhile, there was nothing to do but work, so they might as well get on with it. Perhaps this could serve as a lesson in how to deal with future crises. If there was no immediate solution in sight, it could be most helpful to stay calm and put one's best foot forward. Sometimes only time will tell and it's best to carry on.

Lily Tilman's snake eased toward Eileen Smith's foot.

"Will the class please turn to page three hundred twenty-nine in the arithmetic book and work problems

one through nine—with no help from friends, please. There may not be friends across the aisle when you ladies and gentlemen of the future are trying to figure out your own problems. And there will certainly not be help from friends on the test next Friday."

The class groaned as one animal.

Lily Tilman's snake panicked at the sudden strange sound and sought to wind itself around the nearest object resembling a tree.

"The test next Friday will include the kind of examples found on page three hundred twenty-nine, so you'd best stop moaning and get on with it."

Books were slapped upon desks, pencils raised in battle against paper, and thoughts trained more or less on problems one through nine on page three hundred twenty-nine. Almost all the students were relieved to face a real enemy. It got them away from that nagging question in the back of every mind—including that of Miss Eileen Smith—where was Eli?

Miss Smith felt an odd crawling warmth around her ankle and leaned over with a shriek. Lily Tilman's tree snake had been found.

3

Tater Sims waited for Eli Wilson all afternoon, two days in a row. Tater had met Eli on the mud banks under the Coosa River railroad bridge every day of his remembered life. He remembered other things besides, but they didn't mean as much. The Coosa River flowed slow and mud-yellow during the summer, fast and mud-red during the winter. Summers, Tater waited in the shade, winters out of the rain. Spring and fall he could fall asleep from feeling so comfortable after working the fields all day. He hadn't found any other way to meet Eli in all that time because the Coosa River bridge seemed just fine up until Eli disappeared.

Just the other day they were swinging out on the vine over the shallows. Eli might have come around to-day, before Tater, and then run off and hid to ambush him. But Eli would have swung on the vine while he waited, and the vine would be switching a little bit still. The vine was tied up.

Eli never went in the river alone because he was scared of deep water, so he wouldn't be swimming in the Coosa. It was swollen up hard from the rains. The train was due soon so he wouldn't be up on the bridge. A half-sunk sun cast shadows across the water. Tater waited for another hour, then he covered the woods. Eli was quiet, but nobody got by Tater in the woods.

Tater was born in the woods. His mother got the birth pains while the preacher was dousing her and she walked out of the water and lay down in the woods and had Tater. One of the women came and helped her— Burlene. Burlene was part Indian, part black, and good at delivering babies and healing. When Tater's mother died, Burlene kept Tater alive on potato-and-water gruel mixed thin. He was one baby determined to stay alive, she said, potato gruel and all.

But Eli was a different story. He was born with a silver spoon in his mouth. Come to think, though, an old black woman fed him, too. There wasn't all that much difference. And they had gathered by the Coosa River bridge every single day, those two old women, Betty and Burlene, with those two baby boys, Eli's the only white face there but nonetheless loved. Then later on, just the two boys met, because they were used to it and seemed like family even after old Burlene and Betty quietly passed on from this life to the next. Sometimes Tater still felt the presence of the two old women nearby.

The leaves crackled and Tater whirled around. He'd

been paying no mind, staring at the water, thinking of Eli. Eli never missed a day, much less two, but here came his old dog, snuffling along without him.

"Sandy Old Boy?" said Tater. Sandy Old Boy snuffled over.

"Where's Eli?" Sandy wagged his tail, slow and sure, like he could help out. Then he just stood there with his tongue hanging.

"Where's Eli? He's not here. Where's he gone? What happened to Eli, Old Boy? Did he send you here?" Sandy wagged his tail a while longer and then sat down on it.

"Come on, boy. Let's walk down the road and meet him. He must be on his way." Tater scrambled up onto the road and Sandy dragged up after him, but they walked all the way to Eli's house without sight of Eli. The house stood high and white against the high white sky. It was the richest house around and after watching it a while, Tater kicked a rock on home, just like Eli always did. No good knocking on that door.

Maybe Eli would come tomorrow. Eli would come tomorrow and say how come he couldn't be at the Coosa River bridge like always. Tater looked back over his shoulder. He had an uneasy feeling of being followed, without hearing any footsteps.

Behind Tater flickered a sharp patchwork of shadows. The thin ghost of Burlene, who had raised Tater, skimmed through briers where no boy could walk. Betty's ghost flickered along behind with no trouble at all. When they sensed Tater's fear, they fell back.

"I've got to tell him about Eli," moaned Betty. "I've got to help some way."

"What can you do?" Burlene sighed. "If you show yourself to Tater, you're liable to scare him out of a year's growth."

"Then I'm going after Eli."

"You know how hard it is to leave the place you're buried, Betty. And you know a ghost's not much help to the living."

"Eli must still be alive," Betty replied. "We'd know it if he died." They swirled and worried through the scuppernongs. They fussed through the saw grass without a rustle.

Back home, Tater blew up a fire from the coals in the stove. He mixed up a batch of cornbread and cooked bacon, and the smell of them both together sent his stomach hungry and aching to eat. But something in his mind ached, too, something bothered and worried the back of his mind all the time his stomach was fussing to get at the food.

Eli had been acting real funny lately. He'd go quiet all of a sudden right in the middle of things and not say another word till their time was up. Tater would talk to him, Tater would even punch him, sort of trying to wake him up. Seemed like Eli must be thinking about something else all the time, just like Tater hadn't noticed when Sandy Old Boy walked up on him in the woods. Where'd he go, Sandy Old Boy? Still outside the door?

Tater walked out to check and there Sandy sat, tongue hanging, watching Tater's shack like it was some high white house on the hill. Picked himself up and walked in the door without a by-your-leave like he lived there and then sat down on his tail again.

"What's up? Go on home, you old dog. I'm not giving you no bacon and no cornbread. It's all for me. What do you think? You're a friend of mine, come high and mighty for dinner? You didn't work no field today. You never worked hardly a day in your life. What do you want, anyhow? Where's Eli, boy, where's Eli?"

4

Lily Tilman squirmed around on the bed until the sheet twisted her up in a hot-weather knot.

"Where could he be, Ma? He hasn't brought the paper by for two days. Folks say he's disappeared."

"Lie still."

"Tell the boys to stop hollering, Ma. Don't you ever get tired?"

"I am tired."

"I'm tired of getting picked on. Those kids in school are all snotty, 'cept for Eli."

"Lily, no telling where Eli is. I told you not to set your heart on that boy for a friend, anyway. Those Wilsons are proud. They won't let the likes of you near them. All they see when they see you is poor white trash. They don't know a lily in the field."

"Eli's not proud."

"Eli's lonely. Lonely don't know proud. You can walk down a road and kick a rock and hit it right on target, but your toe hurts all the same. Eli's toe's hurting from all the rocks he's kicked down that road."

"Eli's not lonely. He's got me—and he's got Tater."

"Not you and not Tater will ever walk through the door of his house."

"When he's grown up we will. You wait and see. Just his daddy won't let us in now is all."

"Lily, Lily, don't set your heart on that boy, I'm telling you again and for the last time."

"I miss reading the newspaper."

Every day since the day she had picked up the newspaper from Eli's backyard and old Henry Wilson had hollered at her, Eli Wilson brought her the newspaper. Every night for years, after his father had finished it and folded it beside the trash, Eli quietly disappeared down the road to catch fireflies and bring Lily the newspaper.

"Aren't you too old to be catching fireflies?" his father once asked with his eyes narrowed up like the end of a whittling stick. Then Eli's excuses shifted from fireflies to frogs, to catfish by flashlight, or just plain walks. But he always disappeared for a little while after dinner. It was such an old habit that his father in the high white house didn't notice anymore. For Lily, getting the newspaper from Eli was as regular as the sun going down, and just as nice a sight.

"You reckon he's hurt somehow?"

"I don't know, child. We'll find out tomorrow, no doubt."

"What's that noise?"

"Night noises."

"No, really, Ma, something at the door."

"Sounds like that raccoon scratching around. Wait a minute, I'm going to scare him good."

"Ma, don't hurt him."

"He's picking at the garbage and dragging it all over the yard every night. I'm going to chase him off."

"Wait for me, I'm coming, too."

"Well, don't get your pity up, it's just a rascally animal."

"Ma, stop, it's not, it's a dog! It's Sandy! Sandy Old Boy, what're you doing here? Where's Eli? Where's the paper, Old Boy, where's Eli?"

Sandy sat down in the red dust and rested with his eyes on Lily like a mirror to her question. He was a polite dog, and he had finished Eli's day as best he could the same as they had done it together just about every day since Sandy was a pup. But where was Eli?

5

Tater and Lily met under the Coosa River bridge and looked at the still vine hanging from the giant tree limb over the river bank. A high white sun lit up the water.

"Where you reckon he is?"

Tater looked at her and shook his head. He was not used to talking to Lily, not used to talking to anyone at all, and he had no answer to give.

"We might should try and find out. Reckon we knew him better than anybody else. Maybe we could think on it together. His pa sure won't be talking it over with you or me."

Tater grinned at her a little. He knew from Eli that Lily Tilman was a fair girl, but her being white and female and with such a big family and all, four little brothers at least, he had stayed away, even though they sometimes worked the same fields. It was not hard. Tater drew a circle around himself, and only Eli had ever been inside it. On account of Betty and Burlene wanting a good gossip every afternoon, they'd dumped their two baby charges together before Tater ever got old enough to close his circle up. So Eli was his friend—what Eli did with other friends was his own business.

Lily, on the contrary, was not wary of Tater. She had too many brothers not to speak right up. She was not wary of anybody, but she respected Tater's circle.

"Eli say anything to you before he disappeared?"

Tater stared into the woods. "He didn't say nothing, and that's the thing. There was something he didn't say, bothering him. I could tell."

Lily thought about that a little while, and Tater liked the way she thought about it, just standing there real quiet. She was so thin standing there in a raggedy brown dress, she could have passed for a tree. He was so busy thinking that, that he didn't at first see Sandy Old Boy rounding the bend of the railroad track. Sandy was just about over their heads on the bridge before either Tater or Lily looked up and saw him silhouetted against the sky. Both of them kind of jumped.

"Sandy Old Boy, you come on down here," Lily hollered.

"Second time you crept up on me," thought Tater. "I must be going soft in the head."

Lily turned to him like she read his thoughts. "That old dog's been following me everywhere I go, just suddenly shows up," she said.

Tater nodded his head. "Me, too."

"Must be looking for Eli, like us."

"Maybe so."

They turned to watch the old hound half scramble, half fall down the steep railroad bed to the riverbank. Then Lily let out a little squawk and pointed her finger. Along the railroad track, strung out in a line, were six other hounds, ranging from meek to mean. It looked for a minute like they were leaning back against the sun, then they jumped down after Sandy to circle Lily and Tater.

Tater backed up a bit. He was not fond of dogs. But Lily stooped down to the nearest one real slow and held out her hand for the acquaintance sniff.

"Lady?" she said softly. Then she turned in the circle. "Favor? Trick? Juniper? Cotton? Sandals? Tater, he's got them all! Sandy's gone and rounded up all the Kings' and Jacksons' hunting dogs. He must have followed us here wanting to track down Eli."

"How come he wouldn't take them to Eli's daddy?"

"Old man Wilson hates this dog. You know how he won't let Sandy in the house, kicks him away all the time. Too raggedy, like us."

Tater blessed her again with the lopsided grin. "Reckon we ought to use these dogs, then, now Sandy's gone to the trouble to round them up. They are kind of mangy looking, but just as long as they can smell out Eli's trail. . . ."

"Let's get on home. You got anything belonged to Eli they could sniff his scent on?"

"I got nothing of Eli's."

"I know what. I got the last newspaper he brought over, wrapped in a shirt on account of the rain. Has his smell all over it and I didn't hardly touch the shirt. We'll stop by and get it and tell my ma."

Lily lit out for home followed by the seven dogs loping along after. Tater dragged on behind and fell out of sight near Lily's cabin.

"Ma?" she yelled out, charging through the door with Sandy Old Boy, Lady, Favor, Trick, Juniper, Cotton, and Sandals hot on her heels.

"Ma, me and Tater are going to track down Eli. Sandy Old Boy followed us down to the river with all these hunting dogs and we're going to get the shirt for them to smell and see if they can pick up his scent."

"Lily, you'll be the death of me. Shoo, dog."

"We got some bread and butter I can take along?"

"Lily, that loaf is the boys' lunch."

"I'll just take a couple pieces, Ma, they won't notice."

"You be careful now, Lily. I don't like this. Those dogs are going to take you on a wild goose chase. What makes you think you could find Eli quicker than the sheriff?"

Mrs. Tilman stood talking to the air. Lily darted into the other room, hauled out the precious paper, all wrapped in its shirt, and made off out the door with bread, some matches, paper, shirt, and dogs.

"Bye, Ma. . . ." Her voice floated back to Mrs. Tilman, who stood shaking her head. "That girl," she said, "that girl is headed for trouble." But Lily was headed straight for Tater, hiding in the trees back of the cabin.

"Where we going to start? I got the shirt, some matches to make a fire, and some food. We might be gone a long time."

Tater nodded and thought a minute. He was not

used to the kind of commotion Lily made. "We can't just mosey all over the countryside."

"The way I figure it, he must have started out from home. Some school kids saw him turn up his drive, kicking a stone like always. And you say he didn't show up by the river after he stopped off home to change his clothes. They've looked all over that direction, so it must be the other one, toward the swamp. But he knows not to go near that swamp. He never goes near that swamp. His daddy would skin him alive."

"All the same, he didn't come to the river. He would've swung on the rope vine, and the vine was still tied around the tree."

Lily scrunched up her eyebrows. She'd heard the sheriff was convinced Eli had fallen in the river and drowned.

"I'm telling you," Tater insisted. "He never in his life passed that vine without taking a swing on it. Plus," Tater looked at her sideways, not wanting to give away any secret of Eli's, "he didn't like going *in* the river that much. Scared of deep water."

"Sheriff's sure been wasting a lot of time, not knowing that," Lily remarked.

"It's his time. Like you said, sheriff's not talking to the likes of me about it."

Lily smiled in her turn. "So you reckon we ought to set out by the swamp."

"Don't know where else to start."

"There's that stretch of saw grass a mile back of his house. Let's take the dogs over there and let them get a whiff of the shirt." The nine of them straggled off in a pack and skirted the high white house—sitting so silent without Eli—by a shortcut through the woods.

"Don't want these dogs getting mixed up. They'll lead us right back up that hill if we get too close."

Tater moved up beside her. Lily kept a pretty good pace—faster than Eli ever went. By the time they got to the saw grass, they and the dogs were heated up in the slanting sun.

"Well, Sandy Old Boy, here's where we're going. Gather around your flea-bitten friends and let 'em have a whiff." Lily held the shirt out for the dogs. They snuffled and capered around, slobbering over it.

"Sic 'em now, Sandy, go get him." The dogs pricked up their ears at the familiar words. There was a hunt on. They fanned out in the saw grass, looking for something. They didn't know what, but when they ran across the same smell as they'd run across on the shirt, they'd know and howl to the world about it.

"Go on, Sandy Old Boy," Lily shouted after their tails. "Go find Eli."

Between the edge of the swamp and the high white house on the hill, Betty and Burlene wailed with worry. They wrung their helpless hands. They strained toward the hounds till the magnetic power that held them near their graves gave way, and they flew after Tater and Lily, into the swamp after Eli.

6

Eli had been hungry ever since he left home. In fact, he had been hungry ever since he could remember, being plump on the outside but hollow on the inside. It always seemed like he needed to fill up on a little handful of something. Betty had made real good pie, and he still missed it. Once he and Tater had eaten a whole chess pie between them and then lain around sick, by the river, moaning. And Betty had fussed at him for taking the pie, too.

Pie seemed a long way off. All he could see was mud and trees. All he could hear was plopping sounds in the water and bird calls and frogs. Moss hung from the trees. There was not a thing to eat in sight, much less pie. It was downright discouraging. Even vegetables would be all right. Bread! Biscuits hot from the oven with butter and honey. His insides caved in.

Cookies. Fried chicken. Mashed potatoes. Lemonade. Chocolate cake. Ripe peaches.

Eli stumbled over a root. He half fell, then lay down the rest of the way. Sunlight flickered over him and lighted up his white-blond hair. The heat sat on his head and the bugs circled around his eyes, smoky gray and sleepy from heat and hunger. It was hard to live up to his purpose. His purpose was to find his mother. He had found a picture.

"What do you mean, 'Who's this?' " his father had asked when Eli showed him the picture.

"I mean," said Eli, "who's this lady in your lap at the picnic?"

His father had stared at the streaked photograph for a long time. "Her name was Sylvia Jackson."

"What do you mean, 'was'?"

"I mean was."

"Is she dead?"

"I don't know."

Eli stared at the picture and something in his head dropped way down into his stomach, which was always so empty and now felt suddenly full of a big unidentified lump.

"She looks . . . real familiar . . . but I never saw her before in any other pictures."

Silence from his father.

"She looks like me."

"You look like her."

Silence from Eli. His father was staring at him with ice-cold eyes. Eli felt like he should never have found the picture, like he'd better go before his father's easy anger flared.

"Did she go away?"

His father nodded.

"How come?"

The wall of silence around his father grew higher and colder.

"She went strange in the head and ran off to the swamp," he said.

"What did you do?" Eli asked.

His father crashed the newspaper down on the table before him. "The woman was a witch!" he roared. "I don't want to talk about her, and I don't want to hear about her. Ever!"

Eli walked away in a daze. His mother. He had a mother. She looked exactly like him. He looked exactly like her. She was a witch.

He could remember Betty, black and warm and comfortable, smelling like chess pie. But before, there was someone else, smelling like gardenia powder—some sort of song being sung and hair tickling his face—holding him close, tossing him high, then holding him close again, rocking back and forth and back and forth again. All this he felt when he took away the picture and stared at it under a lilac bush in the yard. All this made him turn his face toward the swamp and mutter, "A witch . . . in the swamp?"

Sandy Old Boy had meanwhile nuzzled up against him and pushed into his face so he had to drape an arm around him and push to keep from drowning in wet nose. Eli fed him in the shed and then closed the door and wandered off. Food always claimed Sandy's attention. When it was gone, he would eventually squeeze back out through the loose boards. But for now, Eli wanted to be alone. He was dizzy from thinking about something he'd never let himself think about before.

"Sylvia Jackson," said Eli.

His mother. He had a mother. She looked exactly like him. He looked like her. She was a witch. He looked toward the swamp, and for the first time in his life, he didn't want to eat. He wanted to go into the swamp and find Sylvia Jackson. The sun went down and hid behind the trees. It got damp under the lilac bushes and Eli cooled off. He went automatically into the house at the sound of the dinner bell, but he did not eat dinner. His father did not notice.

Later he picked up the paper, which his father had put by the back door, but instead of starting down the road toward Lily's house, kicking a can or rock like always, he wandered toward the swamp. The swamp pulled him, the swamp his father would beat him for stepping foot in.

First it was unfamiliar, and then it was spooky. Dark, with fireflies, and then dark with starlight. Dark with noises. Maybe his father was following him. Maybe his father *wasn't* following him. Maybe something else was following him. Deep into night, he lay in the dry grass patch where he had fallen and slept away the noises. The newspaper seemed a thin pillow on the ground. He woke up with the rising sun and kept heading deeper, straight away from home. The only real fear he had was deep water, but he watched his step and tried not to think about it. He tried to think about Sylvia Jackson, whose smiling picture promised a safe place. All that day, all that night, and into day again, Eli followed the picture of Sylvia Jackson's face, sometimes in circles. . . .

Far away, Lily and Tater floundered after the hounds. They were starting to feel as lost as Eli. In his Wilsonville office, Sheriff Stone rubbed his bald spot and considered whether to make one more search before giving up on Eli Wilson.

7

Sylvia Jackson hovered over the fire, with her hair streaming so close, the wonder was it didn't start burning. In fact, the day was so hot already, the wonder was she had a fire in the first place. But what's a swamp without a fire? There's no boil, no toil, no trouble without a fire. So Sylvia Jackson made a fire every single day of her life in the swamp, even now that her life was turning older. You could tell by some gray hairs that hung so close to almost burning.

Sylvia Jackson didn't mind the heat, she was glad of it. She was warm, peculiar, lumpy, and alone, all at once, and she didn't mind any of it. The only time in her whole life she had ever minded, come to think of it, was being married to Henry Wilson, who kicked animals. And leaving her child to him.

There was absolutely no kicking in the swamp. A body could roam undisturbed for days at a time, nobody kicking anybody. *Why*, do you suppose, *why* would anybody kick somebody else? Sylvia Jackson discussed that with herself over the fire, just out of its reach, and muttered a few spells for good measure. You never knew when a spell would come in handy. That's why she made a fire every morning, no matter how hot it was, because you never knew when a spell would come in handy, and fire helped a spell. She had been feeling, lately, like something would happen. It was just a feeling, just a warning sense. Nothing was really different yet: she collected birds' eggs and ate them in the morning. She weeded the herbs and sprang the traps and slept in the afternoon and poled through the swamp. She banked the fire every night.

But there had been some dreams. And there had been some prickly feelings along the back of her neck, that something different was about to happen. You couldn't know those things unless you'd been a swamp witch for so many years that even a ripple in the water changed the pressure of your thoughts. You woke in the dark. You remembered things, watching the fire.

It was strange to live a life. You never knew what was going to creep up on you. First it was that mean Henry Wilson, long ago. Then it was that sweet baby, shortly thereafter. Then it was the soft swamp. And now it was a quivering feeling that something different was going to happen.

Sylvia Jackson jerked her head back from the flames just in time to keep the gray hairs from catching on fire. The sun was already high. No need to keep the fire up beyond making this one little spell, just to find out what was about to happen. In fact, too much smoke might draw unnecessary attention, though nobody ever came this far into the swamp. The whirlpool scared them off. The whirlpool had drowned a sight of folks who didn't know its ways.

But still, there was no need for unnecessary smoke. You never knew what would find you. Sylvia Jackson had followed hunters for days and watched what they did. It was downright strange what people did to other animals. You could never tell by how they talked, just by how they did. That mean Henry Wilson. That sweet baby Eli. Such trouble.

Sylvia spoke her spell. You couldn't tell what the fire told Sylvia from what Sylvia told the fire, but the fire gave her a time to figure things out. One way or the other, it usually worked. Fire spells allowed for listening to the inside and the outside of things. Witchery was so simple and sure, along with patience, along with a few herbs.

She turned to the cat cuddled by her side.

"Temper?" she said. "This particular fire is not telling me anything. How come I have these prickly thoughts up and down the back of my neck? How come my thoughts are turning in circles with no bottom, just like that whirlpool?"

Temper did not move to the right or to the left.

"What is the meaning of this disturbance in the swamp?"

Temper did not flick a whisker.

"Would you like some egg, Temper?"

Temper leaped to attention.

"You're an old fool cat."

Temper wrapped affectionately nearer. He was slow, but he knew about eggs.

"Temper, take a bite now, it's time to set out. We're late today. The birds have woke and gone."

Temper leaned his face into her hand, filled with egg, and licked up breakfast, licked it clean.

"Temper, that's enough. You'll take the skin off. A body has to keep some skin on her hand. Go and find your own breakfast now."

But Temper would not. He liked eggs in the hand. He sat back licking his own paw and watching sideways while she doused the fire, saving some coals, as always, for dinner. Tonight he'd get meat. That's what marked day from night. Temper was not picky, but he liked things regular. Bird eggs in the morning and meat in the evening. It was natural. Nothing told him any different. There *was* a kind of oddness about his mistress this morning, but that was nothing to pay attention to, as long as there were eggs. He moved to the back claws and spread them out efficiently. Some dirt tucked in there. Disgusting. He licked hard to remove it. There now. Nothing like the taste of bird eggs to win over a dirty claw.

Sylvia Jackson watched him and ran her fingers through her own tangled hair.

"You make a body feel ashamed, Temper, carrying on that way over one bit of dirt in the claw. It's time I took a bath. My mind's been going in circles; it's right we go by the whirlpool. Maybe that's what the fire's telling me. Soak in the creek below the pool today, soak in the deep part below the circles. All I see in that fire is circles. You want to take a swim?"

Temper did not want to take a swim, nor ever did, but he'd go along, stalking in the leaf shadows and pouncing on lizards, hoping they weren't snakes. Temper didn't like snakes. They were a bit large for his taste and served no useful purpose, even to pounce on. He had pounced on one once and almost died from the bite.

"Come along, then, old cat, and let's have a look around. I just wish I knew what was troubling this swamp and what was troubling my mind. I dreamed last night, dreamed of baby Eli, for the first time in years. Where do you reckon Eli is, what do you suppose the child is up to now? Reckon he's calling me after all this time? Reckon he's in need?"

8

With his mother in mind, Eli had come all this way, all this way to the muddy water ahead and the roots that tripped him underfoot. All this way to feeling finally hungry, really hungry. Hungry from not eating for days and nights. He thought about his father waiting for breakfast, Miss Eileen Smith waiting for the class to settle down, Sandy Old Boy waiting for their walk, Tater waiting under the bridge, Lily waiting for the paper. It had been a mean trick, shutting Sandy Old Boy into the shed, but he was being a pest with his cold nose. Though Eli wouldn't mind a cold nose now, or breakfast, or supper for that matter, particularly with chess pie.

Funny, that looked like smoke not too far off. Hard to tell swamp mist from smoke. No indeed, that looked like smoke for sure, big puffs, and smelled like wood smoke with something cooking. Must be somebody close by. It seemed like days since he'd seen a soul. Reckon that could be a cooking fire?

Slowly he pulled himself up off the ground and squished toward the smoke. The swamp water pulled on his feet, long since soaked through. Usually he kept half an eye on the mucky swamp grass, but now he just glanced down every so often and kept his eye mainly on the smoke puffing away, closer now. Up to his ankles he was, up to his knees. He wished this marsh would rise into hard ground. The water was beginning to seep up to his waist. Not his favorite thing, but he could go along in shallow water for a little way, if he had to.

And then as if it heard him, the water suddenly reached at his neck and the ground fell away from his feet. The tattered newspaper he had clutched so long floated away. There was a slow twirl to the water, like a giant muscle, and he was pulled sideways, sucked under. He kept trying to paddle, paddle as hard as he could, but that muscle twisted him under till he got a nose full of water instead of air. Water in his ears, water in his hair, water in his eyes, water in his mouth, water in his nose, water down his throat, water in his lungs. He was breathing water, fighting and paddling and twisting his head but getting pulled under and getting nothing to breathe but water.

The whirlpool grabbed and circled him downward into muddy swamp water. The whirlpool was as hungry as Eli had ever been. It sucked him down till there was nothing left but a pitiful arm, white and crying for help above the muddy water. Eli was not a fighter, like the whirlpool, and the whirlpool was winning, filling up his body. The water closed over his head and made a ceiling. The water closed around him and made a black tunnel. At the end of the tunnel was a light. Now the light pulled him toward it, and Eli was drowning.

"Mother," he thought. "Mother."

When Sylvia Jackson pushed through the bushes by the whirlpool, all she saw was a white hand flopping limp above the dark water.

9

Eli faded out of his body toward the light until it completely circled him and took the shape of his own body. The light boy began to lift upward, loosed by Eli's last breath. The glowing face of his old nurse, Betty, flashed past him, with the bright memory of her friend Burlene. Yet someone else was breathing into Eli, pummeling his body, pulling him back from his light. Just as his lighted spirit broke free, air and water heaved through him and he retched, crying and gasping and clinging to his source of air, the mother who held him. Eli lived again, but his light-twin hovered above and touched Eli's pale, tired hand with pride.

"We are two," whispered Eli's ghost.

Eli flopped weakly in Sylvia's arms. With the strength

of a mother renewed, she dragged him up toward her hut in the swamp. Eli's ghost stayed close, quick as a fly, soft as a snake, twirling and swirling, trying out his new self. And trailing behind him unobserved came two more lighted shapes, Betty and Burlene. Drawn by the power of Eli's entering death, they held one another, hoping for Eli's life, wondering at Eli's ghost.

"I sure like to fly," whispered Eli's ghost. "I sure am glad I'm not body bound." He looked at Eli's limp form. "That is some hard life. Brother, you have set me free, and I'm grateful. I'm going to set you free, too, you wait and see. I am going to lighten your load."

Eli's ghost waltzed through a bush and gave a little flip, causing the leaves to quiver despite the windless heat. He watched Sylvia Jackson maneuver Eli across the clearing in front of her palm-thatched hut. She worked the boy through an open doorway onto the raised platform floor she had built on stilts to avoid reptile visitors and high rains. Eli's ghost saw Sylvia hover over Eli, rub his face and hands, croon and smooth the damp hair away from his eyes. He felt a newborn loneliness. Almost, he yearned to blend back into Eli's body, but he held back and flickered around the clearing, whipping up whirlpools of light and longing for attention.

Suddenly he felt a cool touch on his back and he turned into the smiling glow of Betty. In a flash they overlapped with a ghostly hug. Burlene smiled and nodded and patted them both on the back.

"Bless your heart, Eli," she beamed, "how nice to be with you once more."

"We won't part again," said Betty, holding Eli's

ghost close. "We're together now. And Sylvia's even got her Eli back."

"How fine," said Burlene, "how fine."

Eli's ghost grinned back and wriggled free from their embrace, sassy now they were with him. He dodged away and tagged them and spun into the treetops, glad to be showing off and no longer alone. Betty and Burlene watched him as they had of old, proudly and without much comment. He seemed a touch livelier than Eli ever had. When they settled their weightless shapes on a stone, Eli's ghost began to roam through the clearing again. Their presence gave him a home base. He darted back to peek at Eli, still attended by Sylvia. Eli was beginning to come around, but he was in no shape to play yet, Eli's ghost could see that.

The shadows were lengthening as Eli's ghost began to poke beyond the clearing into the swamp. He found he could brighten and dim. He could blaze up or fade out. When he concentrated on his hands, they got brighter. His fingers would shine one at a time. Probably his ears could appear separately. He could play hide-and-seek with his own feet, disappearing them from each other.

Betty and Burlene relaxed on the rock. They fanned their already cool faces with palm fronds from long habit, knowing Eli's ghost was safe from ever hurting himself. He roamed in widening circles until, from far off, he spotted a flare of firelight in the oncoming night. He darted back once to the clearing, drawn by Sylvia Jackson's crooning, Betty and Burlene's companionable presence. Then he turned to hunt down the fire, and the deep cypress shadows swallowed him up. His light flickered and was gone.

Slowly Betty and Burlene moved to follow him, puzzled by his restless pace and quick disappearance. Eli had been a quiet child. Eli was found. Eli was not only safe, but doubled. Now where was Eli's ghost going?

10

A slanting sun had warned Tater and Lily that it was too late to return home before dark. It hadn't taken long to stop and make a fire as night came on. The swamp ground raised up swirls of white fog in a black night. The frogs hollered at each other across the bog. Lady, Favor, Trick, Juniper, Cotton, Sandals, and even Sandy Old Boy were stumped. They had spread and sniffed, followed and bayed, waded and stopped cold, then come slinking back one by one to Tater and Lily, who were chewing on bread.

"This is one big swamp," said Lily. "A body could get lost forever."

Tater swallowed his dinner and reached a hand out absently to pet Sandy Old Boy. Without rightly knowing, he was becoming fond of dogs, especially this one that followed him around everywhere, this old friend of Eli's.

"Don't look like we're getting anywhere near finding Eli."

There was a loud, rude noise.

"Tater!"

"What!"

"You sound like a bullfrog. Don't burp so loud."

"I didn't."

"You did."

"I did not."

There was a snicker nearby. The fire licked around its branch of wood.

"I did," said Eli's ghost.

"Who's there?"

Sandy Old Boy rose joyously to his feet.

"Eli? Sounds like Eli. Eli, are you out there?"

"You're hearing things, Lily."

"I sure am. I heard Eli, clear as day. Sandy heard him, too. Look at Sandy."

Sandy Old Boy was wagging his tail a mile a minute and jumping around in a circle with his head twisted toward the center. Then he reared up on his back legs and leaned his front paws against the air and danced.

"Tater, do you see what I'm seeing?"

Tater's mouth had come unhinged.

". . . 'cause what it looks like is an old dog standing up to take a walk."

Sandy paid them no heed. He leaped up into the air again and stared rapturously into what appeared to be treetops, with the moon just peaking over their leaves.

"What are you-all doing down in this swamp so late at night?" The voice came from right over Sandy's head, and the voice belonged to Eli. Tater and Lily trembled.

"Eli, Eli, where are you?" Tater cried out.

"Here, Tater, I'm right here. What's the matter with you?"

"What's the matter with me? What's the matter with *me*! Where've you been? Are you hiding? You think this is some kind of a joke? You fooling with us? You come on out. Come out right now or I'll beat your backside!"

"Just try and find it."

"Boys, boys, don't fuss."

Tater whirled around. "Burlene?" He heard the voice of the woman who had raised him. A woman long dead. The swamp ground sent up more white fog, but the frogs were not making a sound.

"You boys shouldn't fuss," said another voice from the trees. "Tater, especially you. Eli's a ghost now and he could make you sorry."

"Lily!" Tater wailed.

Lily sat up stiff.

"Lily . . . ," Tater said again, "this swamp is full of ghosts. Betty and Burlene, can you hear them? And Eli. He must have got killed. Lily? Can you hear them?"

"I hear them plain." It sounded like her four brothers having a real bad day. "Tater," she said, "we might as well be civil. Looks like they're camping out with us, anyway. . . . Eli? What's going on? I really missed you, Eli. We all been wondering where you were."

"I been looking for my mother."

"What mother?"

"I had a mother, Sylvia Jackson. I found her picture and Daddy wouldn't talk about her except to say she was witchy and ran off into the swamp and he never wanted me to say her name again."

"How come?"

"I don't know. It's another one of his dislikes. But I got real hungry to see her. I tried to find her in the swamp."

"What happened?"

"I drowned."

"Drowned!"

"Well, for a little while I drowned. My mother came and pulled me out. Now there are two of us, two Elis."

Tater was turning back to his natural color again. "What the blazes do you mean, now there's two of you? Eli, *show up!*"

"I warned you, Tater, don't get mean with a ghost," chimed in Burlene. "It'll do you no good."

"You stay out of this, Burlene."

"Don't talk to her like that, Tater," said Eli's ghost. Just like some bossy old friend.

"I'll talk however I want to anybody," said Tater, "much less somebody nobody can see."

"Well, but Eli, what do you mean, two of you?" Lily butted in.

"Like twins. When Eli died, his ghost was born, and now there's both of us. Eli's back with Sylvia."

"Sylvia Jackson?"

"She revived him."

"What do you mean? He's dead!"

"I'm dead. He's alive."

"You mean I got to put up with two of you?" said Tater. He would lose at any game.

"Listen, Tater, do you realize what he said?" Lily turned to him with eyes shining. "That means Eli's still alive, and he's with his mother. We've got to find them. Just think, Eli's found his mother. We didn't even know who his mother was. And now we can find them both. He wasn't kidnapped and he didn't fall into the sawdust. He's around here somewhere."

"Quite a ways on," said Betty.

"I don't know," said Tater. "I just don't believe this."

"It's nice to see Betty and Burlene again, isn't it, Tater?" asked Eli's ghost.

"What do you mean, see them?" fumed Tater. "I can't see anybody."

"Really?" said Eli's ghost.

"You can see me, Tater," said Lily.

"You're not appearing hard enough," Betty said to Eli's ghost. "You have to appear harder in front of people. The more unbelieving they are, the harder you got to work at appearing. It's not polite to talk to someone without showing up."

"Still fussing at me," grumbled Eli's ghost.

"I never fussed at you till just now. And I never had to fuss at Eli."

"Can you still cook?" asked Eli's ghost. "I was thinking about pie recently."

"You can't eat," said Betty. "We'd have to find Eli to discuss eating."

Eli's ghost sat down on his heels. Sandy Old Boy crouched down beside him. "Come to think of it, I'm not hungry anymore."

"Now I know you're not Eli," said Tater. "Could you just appear a little harder so we could get a good look?"

"Lord, yes," said Lily. "We don't even know if you're really Eli at all."

"I'm not," he said, sounding annoyed. "I'm once and for all Eli's ghost." With that, a strange white figure, just the color of the light on Eli's white-blond hair, began to glow beside Sandy Old Boy, who sat with his wet nose resting in the light boy's lap.

"Eli!" cried Lily.

"Eli!" Tater sighed.

"Eli's ghost," snapped Eli's ghost. There are two of us. We're different."

"Amen to that," said Betty.

"But where is he, then?" Lily demanded. "Where's Eli?"

"I'll show you," said Eli's ghost. And he and the faintly outlined Betty and Burlene circled the clearing and set off into the swamp. Without a word, Lily and Tater got up and followed by the light of the moon. The six hunting dogs ambled after them. There wasn't any place else to go. . . .

Sheriff Stone reined in his horse. He had debated turning back at twilight but thought he caught a faraway flicker of firelight. By the time he circled a wide bog to get there, all he found were embers, but they sparked him on. Maybe Eli had caught something and cooked it here. Not many folks visited the swamp at night. Maybe the boy was wandering just ahead.

Sheriff Stone spied some broken branches and beaten grass. He took pride in his tracking. Already he could imagine telling about his heroic night ride through the swamp to rescue Eli Wilson. Pity that Henry Wilson would be too stingy to offer a reward.

The night did seem spooky, but Sheriff Stone was a lot braver on a horse than off. He decided to keep going, night or no night.

11

Lady, Favor, Trick, Juniper, Cotton, Sandals, and Sandy Old Boy roared through the bushes. They had finally caught the scent.

"You're a little late," said Lily sweetly to old Sandy's tail, which waved in confusion. Old Sandy had just smelled the person he'd been walking with for several miles. In fact, he felt a frenzy of barks coming on, the howl of discovery, but there was no one to discover. Eli's voice was here beside him. Yet Eli's smell was up around the bend. Sandy Old Boy began to race madly toward the smell, then turned around and ran full-tilt back toward the sound of Eli's ghost talking.

Lady, Favor, Trick, Juniper, Cotton, and Sandals sped through the pines, howling, full speed. They were familiar with Eli's scent only, and it was dead ahead, stronger and stronger. They had passed his brightly lit shape without a glance or sniff.

"Hold up!" shouted Lily.

"Never mind," Burlene chirped in her ear, "we'll show you the way." Lily jumped. She was not used to traveling in the company of ghosts.

"Could you appear a little harder?" she demanded. "I can't see a thing and you're right by my ear."

Burlene lit up. "Is that better?" she inquired.

"A whole lot," said Lily.

"Burlene, I can see you!" screamed Tater, and threw his arms around her waist, hugging himself and almost tripping over Sandy Old Boy, who was weaving in and out of the legs of Eli's ghost.

"There now, there now," she gasped. "How this boy has grown!"

"What about me?" asked Betty. "Don't I get a hello, Tater?" Her bright form lit the path.

"Betty," Tater said. "We're all together again . . . the whole bunch of us."

"Not exactly," snapped Eli's ghost. "I'm new."

Lily was panting along beside them. "Don't be picky," she said to Eli's ghost. "You're lucky to be in on this at all. This is really exciting."

"If it weren't for me, you wouldn't even know Eli's alive."

"You don't even know Eli," said Lily. "He would never go around saying 'If it weren't for *me*.' He's not so high and mighty."

"I told you we are entirely different."

"Well, wait till you get to know Eli. You'll be glad you're his ghost, is all."

"There are certainly a lot of people around here interested in the welfare of Eli."

"He's a good friend."

"Is that why we're all huffing and puffing after him through this wet swamp?"

"That's why."

"You know, you aren't bad for a girl."

"What do you mean by that?"

Betty and Burlene seemed to lift Tater ahead, while Lily was left panting beside Eli's ghost.

"You move pretty fast considering you're not a boy."

"Listen, runt, you do seem to be just about everything Eli ever wasn't. What gives you the idea that girls move slower than boys?"

"Just look at you."

"I'm *human*. You're a *ghost*. You can *fly*."

"That's true; but then, you can't."

"I can hardly wait to see Eli. I got to tell him how bad his ghost is."

There was a soaring chorus of dog voices ahead, and rising above it, the spit and snarl and scream of an aggravated cat. Temper was treed. He spat down from a cypress tree just outside of Sylvia Jackson's clearing and wondered what in the world could happen next. His mistress was acting up lately, but there was nothing to prepare him for this onslaught of slavering dogs.

"Yiaow," he called out to Sylvia.

Sylvia was busy in her hut. She had pulled out the body attached to the hand flopping above the whirlpool. It had appeared to be dead, but she had pumped water out of it and breathed into it. The body had moved,

whereupon she had wrestled it to her clearing and into the hut, rubbing it and fussing over it and staring at it for hours. It could not escape her attention that the body looked just like her. Temper, therefore, ceased to be of concern just now.

"Yiaow," he called again, and it was the last sound Sylvia Jackson heard before the clearing filled completely with dog howling. Lady, Favor, Trick, Juniper, Cotton, Sandals, and Sandy Old Boy leaped after each other and raced about the hut trying to decide whether to pursue a strong smell of cat in the tree or the scent they had been tracking all along from the shirt, which led into the hut. Back and forth they raced, noses to the ground, howling, baying, barking, and yapping.

"Sandy," whispered Eli. It was his first word since drowning.

"Sandy?" echoed Sylvia Jackson in her loudest voice, trying to reach the half-conscious child.

"Sandy," said Betty and Burlene at once from thin air.

"Still alive, and look at him racing around like a puppy. Such a cute puppy back in the old days. Only real family Eli ever had, outside of us," said Burlene.

"Looks like he's acquired a lot of friends," said Betty.

"Looks like."

They swarmed through the clearing: Tater, Lily, Lady, Favor, Trick, Juniper, Cotton, Sandals, and Sandy, with Eli's ghost joining Betty and Burlene as they hovered in the air, and of course Temper up in the tree. Temper did not intend to be included, but then neither did anybody else. They all ended up in a circle, looking for Eli, along with Sheriff Stone.

Sheriff Stone had been led straight to Sylvia Jackson's hideaway by all the noise and had caught up at a gallop on his fancy mare. With one grim look at Lily and Tater and the yowling dogs, he dismounted, tied up his horse, and stepped across the moon-flooded clearing toward the little hut. A second look upward into the three ghosts circling the cat in the tree might have caused him to pause, but instead he bellowed out, "Eli? Are you in there?"

"Drat," said Sylvia Jackson.

12

Eli's face looked whiter than his ghost. He shrank into the bony arms of Sylvia Jackson when the sheriff appeared.

"Sylvia Jackson."

"Sheriff Stone. You just stay out. Your kind ain't welcome here."

"How long you been hiding in this swamp, woman?"

"Long enough to like it."

"Did you take that boy from his daddy's house?"

"I took this boy from a whirlpool, back from the dead."

"What's this about, boy, what're you doing in this swamp? We been looking for you all over the county, days on end. You run away?"

"I didn't run away," said Eli, so soft it was hard to hear. "I come here."

"Reckon there's a pretty small difference, Eli Wilson. I'm taking you back now, you hear?"

Eli's soft face melted in tears.

"No use crying about it. Your daddy's gonna be mad enough like it is. Reckon he'll beat some sense into you, taking off like this."

The sheriff strode across the hut so fast—lifted Eli out of Sylvia Jackson's arms so sure—was back out in the clearing so far—that he almost made it clean onto the horse. Then Eli started to kick and scream. Sylvia Jackson hurled herself at Sheriff Stone like a wildcat. Lily, Tater, Lady, Favor, Trick, Juniper, Cotton, Sandals, and Sandy Old Boy closed in around him in a tight circle, hollering and barking respectively. The horse began to snort.

"You-all back off, now, I got to take this boy back to his pa," said the sheriff loud and slow over the din.

"No!" screamed Sylvia, dragging on his arm. "This is my boy. I lost him once and I near lost him again. I am not losing him now."

"Reckon you should have thought of that a while ago, ma'am, back when you had him."

"I could never stay in that Wilson house. He's not going back there. I want this boy running free"—Sylvia scratched at him—"in this swamp where his father's not going to kick him around."

"The father has custody of the child in a divorce obtained on account of a wife's desertion." The sheriff pointed accusingly at Sylvia. She pointed a long finger back at him.

"You tell them, then, Sheriff, you tell them he's dead. Tell them anything you want, long as he stays here with me."

"Ain't nobody in the world cares about that boy except what's standing right here in this circle. Not a soul in town would waste a night's sleep over hearing the news of his death, Henry Wilson included." This statement floated down among the trees from the direction of Betty's ghost.

The sheriff slowly raised his head. "Who you got hid up in that tree, you crazy witch?" he asked Sylvia.

"Never mind what you can't see," said Eli's ghost, floating down and twitching the sheriff's mustache, "or what you didn't see. You don't even have to lie that Eli's dead. Just go back there and tell the folks that you saw Eli's ghost. I'll even go back with you, to prove it. I'd enjoy to." Eli's ghost smiled wickedly. There would be no shortage of things to do in the high white house on the hill—things that Eli never could, or would, have done.

"That's a real good idea," said Burlene out of the tree. "I always wondered why such a sweet boy as Eli had to suffer such a mean father. Now they're each going to get what they deserve."

The sheriff's head was whirling. First it appeared that a cat was talking to him from the top of a tree and then he heard and felt things close by where nothing was. He backed toward the edge of the clearing.

"You *are* a witch," he whispered to Sylvia.

Eli's ghost hovered after him and twitched the other side of his mustache. "Don't you forget it, either, Sheriff, because if you go spreading tales about Sylvia Jackson's hiding place, she'll hex you so fast every hair on your head will fall out."

Sheriff Stone clutched at his bald spot. "That's not fair."

"It's not fair to send a sweet boy away from his mother," said Betty.

"Would you either shut up or show up?" Sheriff Stone yelled at the treetop.

Betty and Burlene swooped down and lighted up by the sheriff's head. He dove for cover toward his horse, which bucked against the taut reins still tied to a tree. Eli scrambled for safety behind Sandy Old Boy, who stood stiff and snarling in front of his boy, full of teeth and protection. Lady, Favor, Trick, Juniper, Cotton, and Sandals closed ranks beside Sandy.

Sylvia Jackson continued to screech and Eli's ghost plucked at the sheriff's hair, while Betty and Burlene passed their cold damp bodies back and forth through his eyes. "You wanted to see us," they whispered. Temper hissed from the tree over his head.

"No!" cried the sheriff. "Yes! Anything! Stop!"

"Say 'please,' " said Eli's ghost.

Eli looked at him in admiration.

There was a long pause, whereupon Eli's ghost pulled out a gobful of hair.

"Please," said the sheriff.

"And Eli will never be back," said Eli's ghost.

"And Eli will never be back," said the sheriff.

"But you saw his ghost."

"I saw his ghost."

"You go on home now, Sheriff. I'll be along directly." Eli's ghost tossed him the reins of his rearing horse.

The sheriff caught them and came close to flying down the path home where Eli's ghost pointed. It was a toss-up who was pulling harder on the reins, him or the horse.

"Lordy," breathed Eli. "How did you do that?"

"It was easy," said Eli's ghost. "What could he do to me? Poor old sucker."

"Plenty to me," muttered Sylvia Jackson, "plenty to me and mine." She held Eli close and finally noticed Temper, glowering down from the tree.

"Come on down from there, Temper, you're all right."

Temper hissed.

"These dogs ain't gonna hurt you."

"Don't be too sure, ma'am," said Lily, "these hunting dogs are fierce." Lady, Favor, Trick, Juniper, Cotton, and Sandals drew themselves up proudly. Sandy Old Boy tucked in closer to Eli and Sylvia Jackson. Tater tucked in closer to Sandy.

"Who's this?" demanded Sylvia Jackson. "The child's got skin like the night, belongs here in this swamp."

Burlene and Betty laughed softly in agreement.

"He's my friend Tater," said Eli, "and that's my other friend Lily."

"You got two friends, and now a mother. You are a lucky boy."

"I got a ghost, too."

Eli's ghost drew himself up proud as the hunting dogs.

"My ghost," said Eli shyly. "What should I call you?"

"Just call me E.G., short for 'Eli's ghost.' "

"E.G.!" said Lily with a shade of scorn. "E.G.'s nothing like you, Eli. He brags and boasts and quarrels and acts awful. E.G., nothing."

E.G. flew down and pulled Lily's braid. She swatted at him hard but ended up hitting herself through thin air.

Sandy Old Boy snapped at E.G.'s lightning motion and E.G. gave his tail a jerk.

"When Sandy Old Boy dies, you can call his ghost S.O.B.," E.G. snickered.

"See?" Lily complained. "Not worth the space he takes up, not half as good as you, Eli, not half."

"Don't take up half the space," said E.G.

"Eli's been too good too long," said Betty. "It's time he had another half, time he could do what he wants to do and be what he wants to be."

"Run a little free," echoed Sylvia Jackson.

"More than time," said Burlene. "But Eli's so good, his ghost's going to be a rascal. Most ghosts got a little balance, good with bad, like a mirror of the people they've been. This ghost is going to be something else."

"Amen," crooned Betty, "amen."

13

The distant thud of Sheriff Stone's horse had long faded into a rumbling sky lit up with sheet lightning. Summer storms were more bark than bite, a lot of thunder and a little drizzle. Still, several splashes of cool, redeeming rain fell on Sylvia Jackson's head.

"It's a blessing from heaven," she announced. "We been given a second chance." The clearing fell into a strange silence. Children and animals thoughtfully watched nothing in particular. At last Temper climbed down from his tree. He did not care for rain, or even mist, and knew that his one chance for a comfortable night was to get dry.

Sylvia gathered him up and herded the others toward her shelter. Temper curved his claws in the presence of the hounds, but the rain had dampened their enthusiasm along with their tails. They slouched into the far corner of the hut for an overdue rest.

The wind seemed to go out of the night and everybody in it. A real rain set in. Sylvia began to hum. She often hummed at night. Humming filled up the hut. Humming made her sleepy. But she could not get comfortable tonight. There were so many eyes watching her. The girl Lily, fresh and young. The boy Tater, with his guard up. The seven dogs, fourteen eyes all told, in that corner. The three glowing ghosts, another six eyes. And two gray eyes, Eli's. Eli stared at Sylvia till she felt her skin was going to peel off. At last, Sylvia matched him gray for gray. She had many things to tell Eli, but only one of them could settle his eyes. Her humming turned into a mutter.

"You think I didn't think about coming to get that baby boy fifty times every day?"

Eli strained to hear.

"It hurt me so, no one will ever know." Sylvia Jackson hummed and muttered, muttered and hummed. The hounds shifted around. The ghosts flickered. The children kept still.

"Not enough food to keep body and soul together. Not a roof to keep the rain off." Mutter and hum. "By the time I knew the way of catching things and finding things and growing things and making things, I got to thinking about how he'd be stuck out here by his lone self with no other body to talk to." Mutter and hum.

"I didn't have much chance at schooling myself. Us Jacksons worked the fields. I don't rightly know what possessed Henry Wilson to pick me but my bright hair

and songs. Reckon he thought of me as his one big failing." Sylvia began to chew on some stray ends of hair.

"Me, I could barely manage to read the newspaper Henry Wilson had delivered to his house every day. Here's this child could have the whole world delivered to his doorstep up on that hill. Am I the one to take him away?" Sylvia began to rock back and forth, hugging herself and staring into the cypress trees.

"I sneaked back sometimes. I spied. Betty was good to you. Betty loved you like her own." Betty nodded from her perch. "You ate good and learned good. What could I do for you in this swamp, besides sing and chant, and you too old for lullabies?" Tears slid onto her chin. The rain slid down the roof. Slowly, Eli edged over to her, laid his head on her lap.

"You're never too old to cry, Eli, and never too old to try. My mama used to tell me that. That's what mamas are for, I guess, even when they can't give you much else."

Tater stayed very still with his legs crossed on the floor and his face closed up. By and by he felt a soft breeze brushing his tight-sprung hair. Burlene wreathed around him, lit up. When Eli raised his head, he saw the brightness and Tater's tight eyes.

"First you had none, and now you got two," Eli said softly to his mother. She leaned over and met Tater's frown head on.

"Good company," she said, "good company."

"What about me?" said Eli's ghost. He lighted his ears up and practiced wiggling them.

"You're not much company," said Lily. "You think you're the cat's meow." Temper licked a paw disdainfully.

76

Eli's ghost darkened his shape and directed some rain-water leaking through the hut onto Temper's carefully groomed fur. At the touch of water, Temper leaped into the air two feet straight up and landed on a nearby hound. There was brief bedlam.

When all the eyes had rearranged themselves, Lily's, Tater's, Eli's, and even Sylvia's began to close. Temper's and the three ghosts' winked greeny-gold toward the roof beams. The hounds took turns keeping an eye on the cypress trees all night. You never knew what might creep up on you.

14

Midnight to dawn hardly seemed like a nap to the thirty sleepy eyes in the hut. Still, when the sun steamed up, it was hard to sleep. For one thing, it was time to eat. Temper in particular was ready for eggs. The dogs were ready for Temper. Sylvia woke up to find fur flying, three children whining, and three ghosts too dim to distract anybody's stomach.

"Lord have mercy," muttered Sylvia. "It's enough to make a body's head spin." Yet she proceeded to produce breakfast, from one hoard or another. The hounds picked up the smell of raccoon and bayed off through the bushes. Sylvia set out to take her bath at last, with Temper picking his way delicately behind. Lily, Tater, and Eli sat around at loose ends. Smoke swirled up from the coals of Sylvia's morning fire. The day was heating up hard. They felt like their bones would melt.

"Let's play hide-and-seek," said Eli's ghost. He darted down from his perch on the roof, where Betty and Burlene were recalling all they'd seen the day before. Every time they came to Sheriff Stone, they fell to cackling.

"I declare," Betty said. "Did you see the look on his face?" Burlene rolled her eyes and wound herself up to start over again. For the first time in years, they had a new memory to mull over.

"This story is going to be a whopper," said Eli's ghost. "Come on, let's play. I'll make it easy. You three can be It. I'll go hide and you can all try to find me." E.G. hovered for a moment in the air beside them and then disappeared without a trace.

"Hey, you're cheating." Eli's sunny face clouded over. "You got powers we don't have."

"Three against one!" yelled E.G. right into Eli's ear. The three children saw a breeze whip past the grasses, then all was still. Tater shook his head.

"He sure is bossy," said Eli.

"And mean," said Lily. They sat for a minute, straining to see some flicker of light among the dark trees. Nothing showed up but a few fingers of hot sun reaching for them through the branches. A spiral of bugs, centered around the beams of light, buzzed their eyes and ears and noses and necks.

"Let's get moving," said Lily. "Maybe we can catch him lighting up without meaning to. Sometimes he forgets his feet."

"Hold on," said Eli. "Let me think a minute. He's not the boss of me. If it weren't for me, he wouldn't even *be*." An unusual, sly smile lit up his bug-bitten face. He leaned over and whispered to Tater and Lily. They

looked at Eli amazed, then scattered through the under-
brush. When they came back to the center of the clearing
where Sylvia had banked her fire, each carried a handful
of twigs and sticks. They began to spark the coals with
dry leaves and bark, muttering something over and over,
just as Sylvia had. Sweat streamed off them as the flames
shot up. Smoke and bugs stung their eyes. They backed off
and stared at their handiwork.

"Now," said Eli, "start out real quiet so he'll come
close." He held up his finger. The three took a breath
and chanted together softly.

> "Eli's ghost,
>   Come and boast,
>   Toast and roast.
>   You're commanded by your host
>   To show whatever you love most."

Eli's ghost sidled toward them through the cypress
trees, still invisible. He had been watching them, but he
couldn't quite hear them. They didn't seem to be looking
for him. They were chanting something. The chant got
louder. Then it reached Eli's ghost and spiraled around,
pulling him toward Eli. He felt compelled to light up,
first his head, then his hands, arms, shoulders, chest,
trunk, legs, and finally, feet.

Eli strolled over and tagged the lighted form of his
twin. "You're It," he said. "Now either you play fair with
me, or you don't play."

Eli's ghost stood blazing, his scowl bright enough to
burn. Then the faintest shadow of a smile pulled one side
of his mouth up, and he turned his face toward a tree.

"You suckers better hide," he shouted, and the three shot off like quail in different directions. "One, two, three. . . ."

After noon, Sylvia came back from her bath with a catch of fish to cook. The ghosts of Betty and Burlene were shady with napping in the hut. The hounds were wending their way home.

"Looks like those children built this fire back up," Sylvia muttered. "Now why in the world . . . in this heat . . . anyway, it's ready for the fish. I'll just lay them on here, Temper, lay 'em on the coals. These here are cat-fish, Temper, nice fat ones, named after you." Temper licked one side of his paw to spiff up his whiskers. It was so embarrassing to drool.

When Sylvia rounded up the hiders and the seekers to eat, Tater brought with him a shirt full of wild figs he had found for dessert.

"Fine," said Sylvia, "fine, ripe figs. But this shirt now . . . tomorrow you-all are going down below the pool to take a bath with me," she said. Tater grinned and buttoned his shirt back on. Eli frowned.

"I can't swim," he said.

"If you can learn how to read," Sylvia said to Eli, "you can learn how to swim."

"I'll help," said E.G.

"You'll behave yourself," said Sylvia.

"I got to go home," said Lily. "My mama's going to fret herself silly with me gone. She'll be headed for Sheriff Stone directly."

Sylvia nodded. "But you got to come back and visit," she said. "Tater?" she asked.

"Reckon I'll stay and take a bath," Tater said.

Eli whooped and leaned over to slap Tater on the back. Quick as lightning, Eli's ghost slipped a fig between Eli's hand and Tater's back. It squashed flat with a sticky splat. Eli whirled around and just missed punching Lily as Eli's ghost dodged behind her.

"Lord have mercy," said Sylvia, gathering up her walking stick. She clucked for Temper. "Come on, old cat, we're showing Lily the way home."

The three children stood in a circle and stacked their hands. Eli's ghost drew near, laying his lighted fingers on top, and they said good-bye to Lily. Betty and Burlene glided down to wave at Lily as she and Sylvia set out, then turned to watch over the boys and Eli's ghost, who had already started to squabble.

15

"What do you say to the fire every day?" Eli asked Sylvia.

"Different things. Today I was mainly thankful for you boys and fixing to take you down by the river."

Eli picked up a piece of charcoal and began to draw across the rock he was sitting on. "Eli," he wrote. Tater stopped beside him and wrote "Tater." Sylvia walked over and stared at the wide, flat rock. She took the piece of charcoal from Tater and slowly, laboriously began to write, "Sylvia."

"You know what we could do?" said Eli. "We could have school right here in the swamp. We could write a new word every day, just like Miss Eileen Smith does."

"Who's going to teach us?" asked Tater. Sylvia dropped her eyes.

"Well," said Eli, "we could get some books and learn ourselves."

"Schoolbooks are boring," said Tater.

"No, I mean the ones with stories," said Eli, "and pictures and maps and stuff."

"Besides," said Tater, "where would we get books, anyhow? If we show up anywhere around here, you'll be hauled back home."

Eli looked stricken. Sylvia doused the fire. "Come on, you children, time to get cleaned up. Maybe we can sneak out of here without E.G. bedeviling us. He's off frog hunting, fixing to find him a champion jumper. Says he'll be winning bets off you-all before tomorrow."

The three of them slipped out of the clearing. There was no sign of Eli's ghost. Sandy Old Boy checked to see that Eli was coming and then raced ahead along the path Sylvia had worn to the creek below the whirlpool. Temper picked his way between Sylvia's legs, offering her the choice of either tripping over him or picking him up for a ride on her shoulder.

Tater and Sandy Old Boy hit the water running.

"Well, that's one way to get a shirt clean," said Sylvia. "Come on, Eli, you're next."

Eli hung back.

"It's not the whirlpool, son," Sylvia said gently. "It won't take you down. Just go in slow till you get used to it and look around for crayfish. We'll think about swimming tomorrow." She waded into the water herself. Temper leaped back to the shore with an offended screech.

Eli threw a stick into the water for Sandy Old Boy to fetch and walked in slowly up to his knees. The water was lukewarm, but cooler than the hot air. Eli squeezed his toes in the muddy bottom.

"Hey, I bet there's a lot of fish under that rock shelf over there," called Tater. Sylvia nodded her head.

"Seems like Tater can smell a fish," said Eli to Sylvia. "I never figured how you caught more fish than me, Tater."

"If you didn't catch 'em, you still got dinner."

"Not anymore," said Sylvia. "We got to fish and we got to scrounge, and that's the truth of it."

"You ever do any trapping?" asked Tater.

"I get by without."

"I done some trapping," said Tater. "Sold some skins, too."

"I got few needs, Tater. But now, with you boys, I don't know. Reckon I could use a needle and thread, for one." She eyed Tater's torn shirt.

"Where you gonna buy and sell, anyhow?" asked Eli. "Like you said, we can't be seen around town." Eli struck the water with the flat of his hand so it sprayed over Tater's head. Tater ducked and dived under the water to grab Eli's legs.

"Help, don't pull me under, Tater! Sylvia!"

Just as Eli pulled away, Tater let him go, so he flipped flat on his back. Sylvia put her hands under him and held him steady above the water.

"Hey, lookit, Eli's floating!" yelled Tater.

Eli lay scared stiff, but Sylvia's hands and the water held him up, cushioned him. Slowly his body relaxed and he drifted on the water that had always terrified him, that had almost drowned him. Now with Sylvia for safety, the water seemed soft, almost comforting. Sylvia eased her hands away, and still he floated. Tater admired him a

while and then started a tug of war with Sandy Old Boy over the stick.

Eli didn't realize he was holding his breath until he started breathing again. Still, he didn't sink. He drifted. As he looked up at the hot blue sky through a pattern of leaves overhead, he thought he had never been so happy since he was born.

"How big is the swamp?" he asked Sylvia softly, still cradled by the water.

"Miles one way and miles and miles the other. Wilsonville's on this side and it's days out the other way."

"We could stay here forever," said Eli.

"Reckon we could travel, too," said Tater, looking down the river. "The creek joins up with the rivers right down to the coast. We could build us a boat, Eli. Nobody knows us in the city. We could come and go and get whatever we needed."

"Maybe," said Eli. "Maybe someday."

"Boy's got to learn to swim first, before you take him on any kind of boat," said Sylvia. "Water's way over his head in those rivers, way over."

There was a rustling in the bushes by the river, and suddenly a huge, soft, dark-green frog sailed over the bank, smack onto Eli's forehead. Eli doubled up in surprise, got a mouthful of water with frog foot mixed in it, and came up spluttering, just a little too deep to put his feet down.

> "Frog, frog,
> Frog in a bog,
> Flying through the air
> And landing on a log.

"That'll teach you to run off and leave me," taunted Eli's ghost.

Eli flailed the water, red-faced and furious, gaining some balance as he moved toward E.G. in awkward, surging waves. E.G. began to back away from the river.

Tater turned to Sylvia. "Eli's swimming already," he said.

16

"Now I lay me down to sleep," murmured Eli, "I pray the Lord my soul to keep. Please keep me safe all through the night, and wake me up in the morning light. Amen."

"Amen," murmured Burlene.

"Amen," muttered Betty.

"Amen," mumbled Sylvia Jackson.

"Amen," said Tater and Eli together.

"Whuff," said Sandy.

"Hiss," said Temper.

They all curled into their own warm corners of the hut. The swamp curled in around them in white swirling hands of fog and tucked in their hut for the night. A soft peace descended on the clearing. It crept through the swamp toward the town, through the graveyard, where ghostly neighbors rose and murmured news throughout the night. It crept past Lily's house, where Lily's mother walked from sleeping child to sleeping child, four brothers and Lily, and smoothed their hair back and their sheets up over their shoulders. Lily smiled but did not wake up.

Then the peace crept toward the high white house on the hill.

But there was no peace for Henry Wilson. He felt uncertain, and he was not often uncertain. He always did what he had been told was right. His mother and father had always worked hard and he always had, too. His mother and father never smiled on Sunday and he didn't either. His mother and father had always kicked animals out of the way, and he always did the same. It was his way of life. If anyone had told him that a person didn't always have to work hard, that a person could smile on Sunday, and that a person did not have to kick an animal every time it got in the way, he would not have believed it. Or he would have believed the person was peculiar.

That was what his wife had turned out to be, peculiar, touched in the head. Sylvia Jackson. He should have known. The Jackson family in general was shiftless and no-account. But at first Sylvia Jackson seemed pretty and pliable. Then it turned out, after they were married, that she didn't like to work all the time. She smiled on Sundays. And she did not believe in kicking animals, ever. And it turned out that Sylvia's child, Eli, was more Jackson than Wilson, the kind who always smiled on Sunday and latched onto every animal he could get his hands on.

Eli had reminded Henry of a little animal, always in the way. Henry occasionally had to whack Eli to teach him a lesson, and one day he even whacked Sylvia Jackson, she got on his nerves so. After that, Sylvia Jackson turned strange and ran away—some folks said to the swamp. Henry Wilson did not try to find her. She was best gone. But Eli stayed, and Henry Wilson just had to get used to him.

That was not easy, because sure enough, Eli had turned out to look just like Sylvia—plump, white-blond hair, gray eyes, and slow-moving. It made Henry Wilson feel mean, every time he saw Eli and thought about his wife, Sylvia Jackson, who had turned out to be witchy. He put Eli away, in another part of the house, with a black maid named Betty, and tried never to see either one of them. Most of the day he was at work. After work he read the paper. After dinner Eli disappeared for a while. And then they all went to bed.

Henry Wilson had long since decided that was the way his life had to be, until the night Eli never came home. Nobody wasted any sleep over it, because Betty was already long dead by then and Henry was certainly not going to waste a good night's sleep. But by next morning, Henry had to report the empty bed to Sheriff Stone, because Eli was a lost child who had to be reported to the sheriff.

The sheriff suggested that they both go and talk to Eli's teacher, Eileen Smith, to see if she might have any ideas. Now there was a woman. Eileen Smith. She knew how to dress, how to talk, how to work. That was clear from how she ran her class. Nobody got out of line. Ever.

The sheriff had asked her all kinds of questions, even tried to kid her a little, and she hadn't smiled once. Very businesslike. The children had kept their heads down every minute, working on their books, without a sound. He, Henry Wilson, should have come to one of those parent nights a long time ago. Eli had never told him what a fine teacher Eileen Smith was. That was just like the boy, always off with his dog, disappearing after supper for a walk. Probably crazy like his mother. It was too bad a man had to be saddled with first a crazy wife and then a crazy son. Now Eileen Smith . . . there was better fare.

Henry Wilson had left the sheriff and walked home thinking of Eileen Smith. A sensible woman. It was amazing how he had passed her in the street all these years and never noticed. She had even come into the store. Strange, how he had been too busy to see.

Eli was supposed to have started working in the store soon. At first, Henry half-suspected that's why he disappeared, to get out of the work. A trial, from beginning to end. Not a thought in the world for his father, not a thought in the world. What was it the poet had said, always mewling and puking? That was a child, all right. What children needed was an occasional whack. His own father had certainly never spared the rod.

Eileen Smith would understand that. Surely it was the secret of her well-behaved class. He would remember to tell her that. He wanted some further discussion with Eileen Smith. It was certainly dead quiet without Eli. The house had always been quiet but never quite dead quiet.

Henry Wilson sat in his chair after dinner at night and listened carefully. Not a sound. No boy, no dog, no servants. The high white house stood absolutely alone, and he stood in the middle of it absolutely alone. After his work was done on Saturday came Sunday. Sunday he

would go to church. Monday he could go to work again. No Eli. No dog and no clutter. Just the cook, and she went home early—until the day Henry decided to seek out Miss Eileen Smith during the cool of the evening. Wouldn't she be happy to come for dinner after a hard day's work? It would be a quiet dinner, completely undisturbed without Eli.

Miss Eileen was delighted to come, and she came back often.

17

A nighttime fog crept once more from the swamp toward the high white house on the hill. With it crept Eli's ghost, restless from his first several months of peace and quiet in the swamp. There was a limited choice of mischief living with three friendly people. E.G. needed some fresh opportunities.

"I declare," said Eileen Smith, "seems like there's a chill in the air."

"Miss Eileen," Henry Wilson called her from habit, "you are too sensitive."

Eileen Smith stiffened slightly at Henry Wilson's words. She did not care to be criticized in any way. Henry Wilson did not notice. Now he was feeling a chill in the air. They sat straight on the sofa, tired from their day of courting but uncertain as to the next step.

Henry Wilson had worked hard at courting Eileen Smith, and Eileen Smith had worked hard at being courted. Henry's sofa was high and covered with slippery material which did not give one a firm grip on the seat. While Henry Wilson's feet reached the floor and he could push against it to stay aboard, Eileen Smith's feet did not, and she found herself sliding forward during the conversation. It was difficult to concentrate. There were long gaps in the conversation.

"The night does seem to have cooled down suddenly," said Henry. He had hoped they were finished with the topic of the weather. But as he looked across the room, the lace curtains blew wildly. "Perhaps a storm is brewing." Henry got up to close the window. It was already closed. He turned to Eileen Smith.

"Miss Eileen, did you notice the curtains blowing a moment ago?"

"Of course not, Henry, the window is closed."

Henry looked strangely at the lace curtains, then went back to perch on the sofa. Eileen Smith wiggled her backside backward in a way she hoped was not noticeable.

"Perhaps you would care for some tea, Miss Eileen."

"That's thoughtful, Henry, but it is getting late."

"Now you stay right there and make yourself comfortable while I bring in refreshments, Miss Eileen."

As soon as Henry's back was turned to leave the room, Eileen Smith felt herself pushed from behind and she slid off the sofa, landing with a thud. Quickly she scrambled to her feet and turned to glare at the slippery silk.

"I declare, it's almost alive," she mouthed at the

sofa. She felt a great temptation to stick out her tongue at the devilish piece of furniture. The chill seemed stronger now. It brushed against her legs like a dog.

Shortly thereafter, Henry tripped and crashed head-long in the kitchen with the teapot in his hands. By the time Eileen Smith found him, he was picking up the pieces and muttering fiercely to himself.

"Henry!" she exclaimed from the doorway. "I heard an alarming noise."

"I fell and broke the pot," he muttered. "There was something underfoot, but I can't seem to find out what it was." He felt the cold chill again; it felt so much like a dog brushing against his legs that he swung his leg back and gave it a kick. His foot landed square and hard against the solid oak kitchen cabinet with a crunch of bones. He clutched at the injured toes.

"That's not the noise I heard, Henry. Listen. It's loud now."

There was a sudden unearthly howl circling the house like a hurt dog. Henry Wilson began to pale. His son's dog had once made just such a sound as a result of Henry's kicking it. The confounded dog had peed all over the rug. Eli had cried for Henry to stop, but Henry was carried away with rage.

"Let it be a lesson to you, boy, never to let that animal into the house again," he intoned. And the cur had dodged his foot and fled. And Eli had looked at Henry with never a word and walked away after it. One thing, the boy had always shown obedience. Better had.

"It is nothing but the wind, Miss Eileen. I'll find the other teapot. A cup of tea should settle your nerves."

98

"*My* nerves," Eileen Smith thought indignantly. But she did not say anything. A small ghost of a grudge had already begun to grow inside her toward Henry Wilson for always criticizing everyone but himself. She was also unpleasantly surprised at the violence she had seen in his kick.

While Henry Wilson fumbled with the tea, Eileen Smith eased with relief onto one of the hardbacked kitchen chairs. At least she would not have to struggle further with the sofa tonight. On the kitchen table, yesterday's newspaper caught her eye and she turned the pages in lieu of something to say to Henry. Newspapers were really so unnecessary in Wilsonville, as she often reflected. They were always too late. One never needed a newspaper to tell what was going on. It was enough just to be sensitive. She herself avoided newspapers.

Suddenly two notices caught her eye, placed much too close together on the page.

"Henry!" she exclaimed. "Have you read this?

" 'Miss Eileen Smith, whom we all remember having taught Wilsonville Elementary School for many years, announced her engagement Sunday to Henry Wilson, Esq., whose family dates back to the founding of our town.' "

"Just so," said Henry, with righteous satisfaction. "But right below is this, Henry:

" 'All hope has been given up for the recovery of Eli Wilson. The boy disappeared some time ago without a trace and has been declared legally dead to prevent future false claimants from appearing to demand inheritance as heirs. Tater Sims, who disappeared about the same time as the Wilson boy and is believed to have conspired in a kidnapping for ransom, has never been captured. Sheriff Stone is quoted as saying the Coosa River Swamp has probably become both boys' grave.' "

"Well, my dear, the matter had to be settled, one way or another."

"But, Henry, do you think it's proper for both these notices to appear together?"

"The fact is, Miss Eileen, *both* matters are finally settled. You are the silver lining to my cloud."

"My, I'm not sure." Eileen Smith rose to bring some sugar to sprinkle in her tea. She returned to the table and lowered herself toward the wonderful, safe, solid kitchen chair. As Henry held the chair for her, his hand—along with the chair—was suddenly jerked back so that Eileen Smith sat smack down on the floor again. She rolled over with a squawk of surprise and a tirade of rebuke at the spluttering Henry.

Eli's ghost blew a kiss to Eileen Smith's backside and flitted away. He hadn't even appeared to anyone yet outside the swamp. Tomorrow would be his first day of school. Afterward, he could visit Sheriff Stone. There was so much to do.

Epilogue

It was a shadowy dawn when Eli slipped toward the edge of the swamp, toward the trees that bordered the saw grass leaning against the hill where he had lived in the high white house. Betty and Burlene hovered back where they'd camped with him the night before, lighting the dark around his blanket roll.

Eli stopped well back out of sight and looked long at the hill. Nothing moved. Then the last lightning bug startled the leftover dark, and Eli's eyes caught a flutter of movement not ten trees away. His heart tightened as it always did when he came too near the hill, but a low bobwhite whistle carried clear, and he answered. With a wave of her hand, Lily stepped toward him, clutching a bundle of newspapers, snitched each evening from the very jaws of Henry Wilson's trash.

Eli and Lily talked the sun up. When Lily turned to go, Eli caught her hand and thanked her for the Wilsonville news. Then, with a ghost of a smile playing on his face, he tucked the newspapers under his arm, squared his round shoulders, and stepped back through the dew-jeweled bushes of the swamp.